For Clay and Louisa —R. M.

To Rose Day, for putting up
with the five of us —L. D.

First published in the United States of America in 2009 by Walker Publishing Company, Inc.
Visit Walker & Company's Web site at www.walkeryoungreaders.com

For information about permission to reproduce selections from this book, write to
Permissions, Walker & Company, 175 Fifth Avenue, New York, New York 10010

Library of Congress Cataloging-in-Publication Data
Morris, Richard T.
Bye-bye, baby! / by Richard Morris ; illustrated by Larry Day.
p.   cm.
Summary: Felix does not like his new baby sister and thinks his parents should take her back,
until a trip to the zoo makes him realize that she might not be as bad as he thought.
ISBN-13: 978-0-8027-9772-8 • ISBN-10: 0-8027-9772-5 (hardcover)
ISBN-13: 978-0-8027-9773-5 • ISBN-10: 0-8027-9773-3 (reinforced)
[1. Brothers and sisters—Fiction. 2. Babies—Fiction.] I. Day, Larry, ill. II. Title.
PZ7.M82862Bye 2009   [E]—dc22   2008044318

Art created with pen and ink with watercolor and gouache, on watercolor paper
Typeset in Memphis
Book design by Nicole Gastonguay

Printed in China by SNP Leefung Printers Limited
2 4 6 8 10 9 7 5 3 1 (hardcover)
2 4 6 8 10 9 7 5 3 1 (reinforced)

Bye-Bye, Baby!

Richard Morris • illustrated by Larry Day

Walker & Company
New York

The day his baby sister was born, Felix was sent to the playground with his sitter. His best friend, Poncho, came too.

"I don't like my baby sister," Felix said to Poncho.

Climbing up the slide, Felix
slipped and bruised his chin. He
cried until Poncho made it better.

When Felix's mother came home from the
hospital, she said, "Say hello to your baby
sister."

"Bye-bye," Felix thought.

WHAAAAAAAAaaa

That night Felix's baby sister went to sleep very late.
Then she woke up very early.

"This isn't working out," Felix said to Poncho.
"I think we should take her back."

The next day Felix's mother was tired. And she had a headache.

Felix knew just what to do.

"Who needs a doctor when we have Poncho?" she said.

When his baby sister was old enough
to walk, Felix's family drove to the zoo.
Poncho came too.
But they no longer had the backseat to
themselves.

At the zoo Felix saw many animals.

He saw an elephant.

"That elephant's so big," Felix said to Poncho, "it could sit on my baby sister!"

He saw a hippopotamus with a mouth
so wide . . .
"It could eat my baby sister!"

And a giraffe with a neck so long . . .
"It could put my baby sister in a tree,
where she would live all alone and then
we would never have to see her again!"

Felix loved the zoo.

He loved it so much that he didn't want
to leave.

Ever!

On the ride home Felix cried.
And cried.
And cried.

WAAAWAAAA

His parents tried everything to get him to stop.
They tried a sippy cup, a box of crayons, and a lollipop.

They even tried yelling at each other.

But nothing worked.

Until . . .

. . . Felix's baby sister reached
down and picked up Poncho. She put
him in Felix's lap.

And that was just what he needed.

"Poncho is still my best friend," he thought.

"But I guess I can call off the hippo."